For Sean,
you Everlasting Gobstopper, you
—B.B.

Copyright © 2019 by Brigette Barrager

All rights reserved. Published in the United States by Random House Children's Books,
a division of Penguin Random House LLC, New York.

Visit us on the Web! rhcbooks.com

Educators and librarians, for a variety of teaching tools, visit us at RHTeachersLibrarians.com

Library of Congress Cataloging-in-Publication Data is available upon request.

ISBN 978-0-553-51345-5 (trade) — ISBN 978-0-375-97469-4 (lib. bdg.) — ISBN 978-0-553-51346-2 (ebook)

Book design by Nicole de las Heras

MANUFACTURED IN CHINA

10 9 8 7 6 5 4 3 2 1

First Edition

Brigette Barrager

VLAD THE RAD

Random House 🏠 New York

Hi, I'm VLAD. I'm a vampire! Here are some things I like: cats, bats, bendy straws, glow-in-the-dark stickers, and bugs. Rocks are nice too.

But you know what I LOVE, more than anything else?

I LOVE to SKATEBOARD!

This is where I learn how to be a scary, spooooooooky vampire. I can find LOTS of things to skate on, in, around, and through at spook school. It's a pretty good skate spot, I guess!

Except skateboarding is not *exactly* allowed. It's not exactly *unallowed,* but Miss Fussbucket sure doesn't like it.

"Skateboarding is a big waste of time!" says Miss Fussbucket. "You need to work on your spookiness. Why can't you be more like your classmates and eerily float to class? Or ooze down the hallway quietly?"

But I HAVE to skate!

When I'm skateboarding, it's like my heart has bat wings
and my feet have wheels!
I feel like sugar-frosted lightning bolts!

"Vlad, this is your first warning!"
says Miss Fussbucket.

Learning to be spooky is fine, but it just
doesn't make me super happy, the way landing
a trick does.

"Vlad, this is warning number two!" says
Miss Fussbucket.

It's hard for me to concentrate on scaring lessons when my brain keeps coming up with *ideas* about stuff I could jump over or through, or tricks I could combine with others to make up new, gnarlier tricks.

Even when I mess up, fall down, and MUNCH IT,
I just get back up and try again.
Skating is not about being PERFECT.

"You'll crack your head open, and your brains will leak out!" says Miss Fussbucket. "Then how will you learn?"

I DO get in trouble a lot. And the worst thing is that I hear my classmates whispering, "There goes *Bad Vlad*. He's such a *show-off*."

I'm not trying to show off, I promise.
It's just that when I'm skating, I am STOKED!
And stoked is the best way to be.

"That's it! Detention!" screeches
Miss Fussbucket.

The blackboard reads, repeated across its surface: *I will not skateboard at school.*

Then it happened.

"Now, Vlad, I don't want to see you skateboarding at school ANYMORE. If I catch you doing it again . . . ," lectured Miss Fussbucket.

And I had a feeling she really meant it.

bard at school.
ard at school.
oard at school.
oard at school.
oard at school.
ard at school.
oard at school.

I will not skateboard at school.
I will not skateboard at school.
I will not skateboard at school.
I will not skateboard at school.
I will not skateboard at school.

I don't know why being spooky and skateboarding can't
go together. Just because Miss F doesn't think so?
If they are both things I can do, MAYBE I can do them at
the same time. . . .

When we took a field trip to the natural history museum
to look at old bones, I was trying to be on my best behavior.
I REALLY REALLY REALLY was.

Until I saw something that gave me a frightful *IDEA*.

"Oh NO!" Miss Fussbucket squealed from way down below. "Don't you dare!"

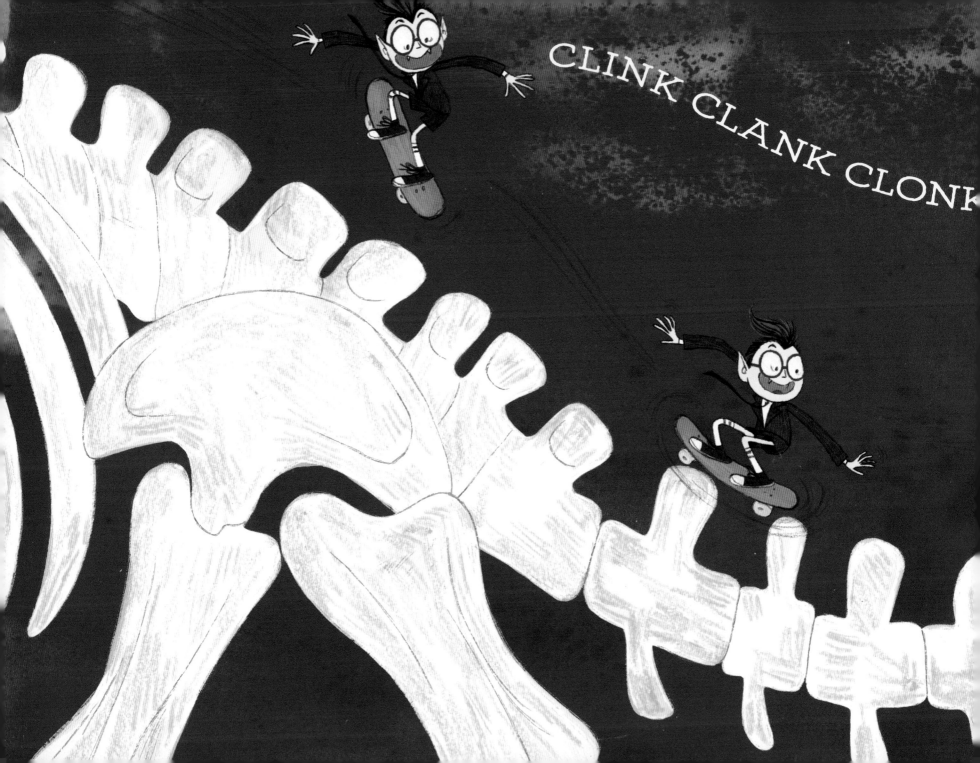

CLINK CLANK CLONK

Those dinosaur bones made a TERRIFYING sound as
I skateboarded down the back!

CLONK CLINKY CLANKY CLONK CLONK!

It was awesome.

When I got to the end of the tail, I hissed and
screeched and ollied right over a pterodactyl!

"A specter!"

"A ghost!"

"A terrible monster!"
screamed all the people.
And they ran away!

Then I SUPER slammed into the woolly mammoth.

"Vlad," said Miss Fussbucket, "you were *radically* terrifying!"

"Vlad the Rad! Vlad the Rad!" cheered my classmates.

And that's how I (almost) stuck my
biggest trick yet and became . . .

VLAD THE RAD!